THIS BOOK BELONGS TO

....

Copyright © 2015

make believe ideas ltd

The Wilderness, Berkhamsted, Hertfordshire, HP4 2AZ, UK.
501 Nelson Place, P.O. Box 141000, Nashville, TN 37214-1000, USA.

www.makebelieveideas.com

THE UGLY DUCKLING

Written by Helen Anderton

Illustrated by Stuart Lynch

make
believe
ideas

Reading together

This book is designed to be fun for children who are learning to read. The simple sentences avoid abbreviations and are written in the present tense. The big type also helps children with their word-shape recognition.

Take some time to discuss the story with your child. Here are some ways you can help your child take those first steps in reading:

❊ Encourage your child to look at the pictures and talk about what is happening in the story.

❊ Help your child to find familiar words.

❊ Ask your child to read and repeat each short sentence.

❊ Try using some of the following questions as you go along:
   • What do you think will happen next?
   • Do you like this character?
   • What kind of voice would this character have?

Sound out the words

Encourage your child to sound out the letters in any words he or she doesn't know. Look at the key words listed at the back of the book and see which of them your child can find on each page.

Reading activities

The **What happens next?** activity encourages your child to retell the story and point to the mixed-up pictures in the right order.

The **Rhyming words** activity takes six words from the story and asks your child to read and find other words that rhyme with them.

The **Key words** pages provide practice with common words used in the context of the book. Read the sentences with your child and encourage him or her to make up more sentences using the key words listed around the border.

A **Picture dictionary** page asks children to focus closely on nine words from the story. Encourage your child to look carefully at each word, cover it with his or her hand, write it on a separate piece of paper, and finally, check it!

Do not complete all the activities at once – doing one each time you read will ensure that your child continues to enjoy the story and the time you are spending together. Have fun!

Mother Duck has ten eggs.
The ducklings hatch.
One duckling is different.

Mother Duck calls
the duckling Ned.

Ned's brothers tease him.

"Why am I different?"
thinks Ned.

The ducklings learn to swim.

Ned goes SPLASH instead!

The ducklings learn to QUACK, but Ned says HOOT instead!

Ned feels sad. He takes his sock and leaves the pond.

Ned asks the geese,
"Can I live with you?"

The geese say, "Sorry,
try somewhere else."

Next he asks the frogs.

The frogs say,
"Sorry, there is no room."

Then he asks the magpies.

No ducks
allowed!

They point to their sign.
It says, "No ducks allowed."

Ned stays in his sock.

One day he sees some beautiful birds.

They say, "Live with us!"

Ned is confused.
"Look!" cry the birds.

Ned has an
orange beak,

a long neck,

and white feathers!

Ned is a swan! He lives
happily in his new home.

What happens next?

Some of the pictures from the story have been mixed up! Can you retell the story and point to each picture in the correct order?

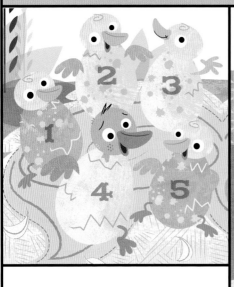

Rhyming words

Read the words in the middle of each group and point to the other words that rhyme with them.

beak

book

look

duck

took

glad

had

sad

home

swan

crash

feet

splash

flash

see

been

beak

sleek

bird

weak

bed

hoot

shoot

root

sock

hen

ten

star

pen

wake

Now choose a word and make up a rhyming chant!

The **hen** counts to **ten** in a **pen!**

Key words

These sentences use common words to describe the story. Read the sentences and then make up new sentences for the other words in the border.

Ned is **an** ugly duckling.

Ned's brothers tease **him.**

He leaves home **with** his sock.

Ned asks if he **can** join the geese.

Then he meets some frogs.

like • very • not

• him • but • with • day • an • can • we • are • up • had •

Next he meets **the** magpies.

He feels **so** sad.

One **day** he meets some new birds.

They ask Ned to live with them.

Ned **is** a swan!

Picture dictionary

Look carefully at the pictures and the words.
Now cover the words, one at a time.
Can you remember how to write them?

beak

duckling

egg

feather

magpie

neck

pond

sign

swan